Under The Mukusu Tree

Stories From Northwest Kenya

by

8th Grade Students

Daylight School

Kapenguria, Kenya

Illustrated by Larry Underkoffler

Edited by Tom Gillaspy

ISBN-10: 1530609453

ISBN-13: 978-1530609451

DEDICATION

These stories are dedicated to all the children of the desert who did not have the opportunity to go to school. At Daylight School, we work to create a Kenya that provides education to all of our children.

CONTENTS

Introduction

Editor's Notes

Acknowledgments

1 How Things Work   1

2 Community   17

3 Do Your Part   33

4 Do's and Don'ts   51

5 Growing Up   73

About The Authors

Daylight School

Introduction:

Michael Kimpur

The nomadic tribes of the Kenyan desert are storytellers. Before my friends had the chance to go to school, we learned as we lived. Our first classrooms were the hills we walked with the cows, the cooking fires where we boiled sweet camel milk, the rivers where we filled our dried squash. Baba's and Kama's - or as we say in English Mom's and Dad's - told us stories of the how the Sun and Moon wrestled to decide who would be queen of the sky. The elder's would gather the children around the fire to tell them about how the Fox and the Giraffe got caught stealing the farmer's grapes.

The students of Daylight School in Kenya wanted to write down these stories so that future generations can read the stories they learned. It is quite a gift because these stories are changing as life in Kenya is changing. More and more children are spending their days learning inside classrooms studying reading, math, and science. They are growing up to do jobs like bankers and lawyers. So they wanted to put together these stories so that the values the village will go with them into their new jobs. These stories teach us honesty, community, and respecting your elders.

Now you might notice that some of the stories are set in a traditional village and others are set in a city and some are set at a formal school setting. This is because our students wanted to add new stories they have heard while living life in the city. Stories that have helped our students translate the village values into 21st Century Kenyan life.

This is how our village adds stories. When elders from other tribes came to visit they shared stories from their village and some of these stories were retold to our children. As each generation comes of age, they retell the stories adding new details to make the story come alive to the next generation. Our community trusts the wisdom of the elders in each generation to translate the values.

Who knows? Maybe someday we will have a story about how the Phone learned about the Internet?

Editor And Illustrator Notes:
Tom Gillaspy and Larry Underkoffler

This collection of stories came about as a result of our time at Daylight School in January 2016. Headmaster Eliud Mungoma asked if we could work with the 8th Grade students on creativity, both in art and writing. Kenyan students take a national exam at the end of 8th grade to determine if they can pass to high school. A rough equivalent in the United States would be a college entrance exam. Part of the exam requires the students to write an original story or essay, graded on grammar, spelling, and penmanship and in part, on creativity.

The students of Daylight School are mostly orphans, very poor, or have special needs and most come from traditional tribal cultures of the Pokot, Turkana, and Karamoja. English is their third language, after their tribal language and Swahili. Being creative in a third language is no small task.

Working with their excellent teachers, Evans Wafula, Christover Nyamwaro, and Robert Poghisio, we asked the students to make journals and decorate them, work on the color wheel, and discuss creative skills under a giant Mukusu tree on the campus. They also read a poem by Kenyan poet Njeri Wangari (Words and Guns) that left all of us with glistening eyes. We then asked them to write a story over the weekend that we marked on Monday so that they could enter the corrected story in their journals.

The stories in this collection are the result. We did not include a couple of stories because they are very personal and extremely tragic. One story is by the founder of the school, Michael Kimpur, who heard it as a child in his home village of Alalay.

All the stories have been edited with the lightest of touch. Indeed some of the stories appear as written. Larry Underkoffler illustrated the stories in the style he used in Kenya, which was so popular with the children. We are all very proud of these students. They are brilliant, excited about education and learning, a joy to be around and **creative.**

ACKNOWLEDGMENTS

All of the teachers and staff of Daylight School deserve special appreciation, devoting a very large portion of their lives to the education of these children. The school would not be possible without Michael Kimpur and the Daylight School Board in Kenya and the Daylight Foundation Board in Minnesota.

More information about Daylight school is available at daylightcenter.org or in Poor Millionaires, by Nathan Roberts and Michael Kimpur that explains how Daylight School came to be.

How Things Work

Everything in the village has a story. As we grow up we learn from our elders where the animals, plants, and humans came from. And tucked inside each story are important life lessons.

The Moon, The Sun and the Stars by Diana

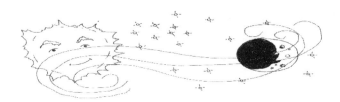

Once upon a time, Moon, Sun and the stars were inseparable friends. They all came out during the day and played and danced until evening, when they went to bed. Nights were filled with total darkness and peace, as Moon, Sun and the stars snored, only to wake when morning came.

Sun, in particular, did not like the morning and would yawn and stretch for a long time before getting fully active, usually around midday. When Sun got tired in the evening, she would start to yawn and get drowsy. Then she would finally shut her eyes in deep slumber.

Since Sun was considered the most beautiful of them all, she was chosen to be queen of all the elements. The decision did not go down well with Moon, who thought otherwise. Moon wanted to be the queen and argued that Sun was lazy in the morning and the afternoon.

After much consultation with the council of elders, Moon was also found to have her own shortcomings. It was discovered that Moon sometimes disappeared completely, which made them wonder aloud how she could rule. The majority of voters considered Moon immature. Poor Moon's bid to rule over Sun was thrown out of court.

While all this was happening in the sky, Moon was forming alliances with the stars and Thunderstorm. She also held talks with Wind. Moon tried to convince them that she was best suited for the job, and that they should elect her come next election.

All this time, Sun was unaware of what was going on and was taken by complete surprise when Thunderstorm and Wind knocked on her door and told her what Moon was scheming. Sun was really annoyed and immediately called the council of elders. The elders advised her that it was best to call a duel between the two of them. The elders suggested that whoever won this wrestling would be crowned queen. The loser would be banished into the night with her partners.

When the day of the wrestling match arrived, every element was tense. Wind, who was to be the timekeeper and referee, was punctual. She made sure that everyone was seated in his or her place. The match began.

Minutes passed and soon, it was hours before Sun or Moon showed signs of slowing down. Wind became tired and called for a break. After the break, the match resumed, but it was soon clear that Moon was weakening. She stumbled and fell after every throw. The wrestling match was finally stopped and Sun declared the winner.

Poor Moon was defeated and she and her accomplices, the stars, were banished to the night. Wind and Thunderstorm, however, chose not to take sides and are allowed to appear anytime they choose, whether at day or at night.

Cloud And Tree by Titus Kiptoo

Long, long ago, there lived two friends. They loved each other as the head and the hair. Those friends were Cloud and Tree. There was no drought because Cloud could produce water and the vegetation was always green.

Cloud could produce water and Tree could produce wood for fires. Tree would produce fruit that the two friends would eat.

One day, Tree did not have enough food to share with Cloud and the grass was drying because only Tree was given water. The animals also did not have enough water for drinking. Cloud and Tree decided what to do so that they could help the animals and grass.

Cloud decided to go above so that the whole land and everything would get enough water, not just Tree. Tree was very worried because his friend, Cloud, was going away. Cloud told Tree that he would come back for visits. That is why clouds come down to the trees and stay there for a period and then go back up to the sky to help everybody.

That is why smoke from burning wood goes up to the clouds. Every tree would be happy if we use the wood for fires. All grass and leaves face up to the sky and horns of the cow remind us that clouds are great friends.

Why Sheep Graze Looking Down by Michael Kimpur

(a story Michael heard as a child around the camp fire)

Cows came to the Pokot people from the sky, given to them by God. Sheep came to the Pokot from the north, over the hills, always following someone else. Goats were always with the Pokot and are wild, and sometimes mean creatures. Cows and sheep graze on grass while goats browse for leaves in the brush.

When sheep first came, they joined with the cows because they like the same kinds of food. The cows would graze about in the best fields and the sheep would go with them, always eating the most tender grass. Sometimes, though, cows would walk a long way to find the best grass. Cows and sheep were always together, eating.

The goats were jealous. They talked to the sheep and pointed out how sheep are so much like goats. They should be together. The chief goat said, "Come to our camp and you won't need to go so far as you do with cows."

The sheep thought this was a good idea, so they left the cows and joined the goats.

The sheep followed the goats wherever the goats went. But the sheep were grazing with their heads up like the goats. The goats didn't like this. You see, goats have a little tail that likes to stand up. The goats didn't like having sheep always looking at their behinds.

The goats yelled, "Why are you always looking at our behinds? Are you making fun of us?"

The sheep, always sheepish, never wanting to have any one angry with them, apologized. And that is why sheep graze with their heads down, never looking up, while goats still browse with their heads, and tails, held high.

Leopard's Kingdom by Dennis Kibet

A long time ago, the forest was filled with many kinds of animals and there was always laughter. The animals really liked celebrations and competitions.

One day, near the end of the year, Leopard, the chief of all the

animals, called a special meeting to plan for the New Year celebrations and wanted suggestions about competitions they could have. Last year, Leopard was angered by Hyena's suggestion. Last year Hyena had suggested a marathon around Leopard's palace and laughed very hard when Leopard came in last. This year, Leopard picked Hare to be the sport advisor.

A week before the competition, Hare went to see Leopard, the chief, who he found basking on a stone outside his palace. He told

Leopard that he had decided that a painting competition for this year would be most suitable. Winners would be handsomely rewarded, but losers would be punished.

Squirrel and Weasel volunteered to paint the animals, for a price. Squirrel knew where to find easy colors and really didn't prepare much. Weasel worked very hard and looked all over for different colors and ways to make the colors brighter and last longer.

On the day of the competition, all the animals came out, one by one, to display their beautiful colors. Tortoise was the judge and everybody looked fine to him. Tortoise had a hard time judging the best, and he put off his decision until afternoon.

Food was served and the animals danced and mingled, everybody having a good time. As the day wore on and the sun shone, with all the dancing, the colors on all the animals began to fade. All except Leopard and others whom Weasel had painted.

All the animals Squirrel painted became furious and turned their anger on Squirrel. They chased him all over the place for cheating them. To avoid being killed, Squirrel and his family darted into a hole between two big rocks. The outraged crowd could not reach him there, but to this date Squirrel still lives in a hole and only comes out briefly to look for food.

Giraffe and Fox by Isabella Chebet

Long, long ago there lived a giraffe and a fox. They were good friends. Whenever they got time, they would sit under a tree near the stream and pass the day happily talking on different topics, telling jokes and really enjoying each other's company.

One day, when Fox was roaming around, he saw some beautiful, ripe grapes growing on a farm on the other side of the stream. Unfortunately for him, the stream was wide and deep, so it was not possible for him to cross.

The following day, Fox met Giraffe and told him about the sweet grapes he had seen on the other side of the stream. Giraffe agreed to take Fox across.

After crossing the stream, Giraffe and Fox trotted into the farm and started eating grapes. Fox gobbled down many grapes very quickly and then patting his full stomach, declared that he was so satisfied he must sing.

"I always sing after having my lunch," Fox announced. "It is my habit." Giraffe was surprised and pleaded with Fox. "Please, please, my friend. Don't sing just now. Let me finish eating first. When we get back to the other side of the stream, far away from this farm and its owner, then you can sing."

Fox paid no attention to his friend's advice. Right away, choosing his favorite song, Fox began to sing. Well, it wasn't long before the owner of the farm heard the music and came rushing over toward them with a BIG STICK. Fox was the first to see who was coming and ran quickly out of the farm, through a hole in the fence. But poor Giraffe was slower to find a way out and when the owner of the farm arrived, he found only Giraffe at the scene of the crime. He beat poor Giraffe until he broke his stick.

When Giraffe was finally able to limp away from the farm, he went to where Fox was waiting for him at the edge of the stream for a lift back to the other side.

Giraffe agreed to carry Fox on his back again, but this time when Giraffe reached the middle of the stream, he had his own announcement to make. "I have a habit too, Fox, and mine is to always

take a bath after having my lunch."

"Oh, no," Fox cried out. "I am very afraid of water. Please good friend," he begged, "before you bathe please carry me safely to the other side of the stream."

But just as Fox had done in the farm garden, Giraffe paid no

attention to what Fox had asked. Right away, he bent his knees and started rolling all around in the water. Poor Fox could not swim, so he sank into the stream and was never seen again.

The Cockerels and The Hens by Prudence

Long ago, the cockerels and the hens noticed that they were the only birds, apart from Ostrich (who was too big to count), that couldn't fly high. During one of their regular gatherings, they discussed this sad fact and decided to do something about it.

"I suggest that we practice flying for an hour a day," said a cockerel.

"No, no," squawked a hen. "We must strengthen our wings first by lifting things using them."

"That will never work," sighed a cockerel. "What we need is help. Let's go to the wise man in the next village. Perhaps he can tell us what to do."

So, they all marched towards the home of the wise man. On arrival, they explained their problem. The wise man had to climb on top of an anthill for him to be seen and heard by the huge flock. When all the birds had stopped clucking and cawing, he began.

"I have a sack here with ten thousand magic beans. Each of you must take a magic bean in your beak and walk home with it. Remember, you must not chatter or open your beaks because then you will lose your bean."

In dead silence, the entire flock began their walk home, each carrying their precious bean in their beak. High in the sky, five giant eagles watched the procession in amazement. "Fools," each eagle thought, and together they swooped down to attack.

"Help!" Every hen and cockerel squawked as they saw the fateful shapes descend. Of course, the magic beans dropped from their beaks as they scurried around in fear.

Ever since, hens and cockerels scratch in the dirt in an attempt to find their magic beans, but none have ever found it. Hens and cockerels can never fly high until they find their magic beans.

Wet All Over by Susan Cherop

Kihunyu was the tallest boy in his class. He was also the most untidy. In fact, Kihunyu was not his real name. His real name was Sango, but nobody ever called him Sango. They all called him Kihunyu.

Kihunyu liked running, jumping and climbing trees. That is why he limped most of the time. He had many cuts and scratches on his body. Children called him "Kihunyu the hyena." They said he looked and walked like a hyena.

Kihunyu did not change his clothes. Most of the time he did not wash at all. He never liked to touch water. The only time he did was when it rained on him or when he got thirsty. When thirsty, he drank it very quickly with his eyes closed.

When he was forced to bathe, Kihunyu splashed water everywhere. He made sure very little water touched his body. So, Kihunyu smelled very bad. He had no friends to play with.

Nobody wanted to sit near him in class. And that was not all. Kihunyu never combed his hair. The nails on his fingers and toes were long and dirty. His bed was always untidy. He never made it. And his room was very messy. Pieces of paper, dirty clothes, and dirty shoes lay on the floor.

Everyone had talked to him about keeping clean. His mother always reminded him to keep clean and tidy, but Kihunyu never listened.

"Sango, clean your room, now!" "Yes, mother, I will." But he never did it. He would instead quickly run out.

Many times he played alone. He was very rough. No one wanted to play with him. When he tried to join other children in a game, they would all move away. This happened to him many times. He felt bad.

Sometimes Kihunyu did not listen to his teacher in class. One day the teacher was teaching math lesson. Some children were playing football in the field. Kihunyu was not listening to the teacher. He was watching the match through the window.

Kihunyu wished he was out there in the field. He liked playing football. The children in the field were really enjoying themselves. Then one scored. "GOAL!" shouted Kihunyu. He shocked everyone. He had forgotten that he was in the classroom.

All the children looked at Kihunyu. He felt like hiding under the desk. He had really made a fool of himself. He thought that the teacher would punish him. He was very frightened. But the teacher just told him to be quiet. From that time, Kihunyu began to pay attention in class. He started doing well.

Kihunyu had many other problems. He ate food with dirty hands. He never cleaned the fruits he ate. He ate dirty mangos, dirty bananas, and dirty oranges. That is why he was sick most of the time. Sometimes he had a stomach ache and at other times a headache. There was always something wrong with his health.

One day, Kihunyu fell ill. He was hot all over. He vomited and his stomach felt very bad. "Mummy, am I going to die?" asked Kihunyu in a weak voice.

"No, my son. You will be fine. I'll take you to the hospital at once." At the hospital Dr. Fariela Mwasi looked at Kihunyu. She felt his forehead and pressed his stomach.

"This boy will be admitted at hospital. He is very sick." Dr. Mwasi called the nurse and then said, "We must give him an injection right now."

Kihunyu did not like injections. But he was feeling very bad. If the injection was going to cure him, he did not mind. He bit his lips, closed his eyes and waited. "There is nothing to fear," said Dr. Mwasi kindly as she gave the injection. Kihunyu felt some pain, but it was not too much.

"Please take me home. I don't want to stay in hospital," said Kihunyu when Dr. Mwasi left. "No, son. You have to get better. Then we can go home."

"But I am fine," Kihunyu thought, but he did not say anything. Later his mother left and went to see Dr. Mwasi.

"I have done some tests on your son. He has eaten a lot of dirty things. That is why he is sick."

"Yes, you're right, Doctor. The boy is very careless about what he eats," agreed Kihunyu's mother.

"I hope he has learned his lesson now," said the doctor. "I am sure he wouldn't want to keep coming back for more injections."

Kihunyu, from that day, began to eat things that were washed and he was also clean. Everybody liked him.

Community

There is a saying in the village: "I am because WE are and, since we are, therefore I am." This means that everyone is connected and everyone has a part to play in village life from the smallest kid to the oldest elder. We all need one another.

Go Away, Goat! By Stella Chemtay

One hot day, Goat went to the lake to drink. The water was cold as it went down Goat's throat. While Goat was drinking, frog jumped out of the water. Frog yelled, "Go away, Goat! You are drinking my whole lake. I was already here. Don't drink while I am here."

Goat said, "Please let me drink. I just need some water to wet my

throat on this hot day."

Frog replied, "Even though you need water for your throat, I don't want you here. I want to take a nap in the sun. I don't want a goat here while I sleep. Now, you have to go!"

Goat shook his head and walked away. Just then, a boy, thin as a pole, walked by. He had a big box. It looked to Frog as though the boy wanted to catch frogs. Frog shook when he saw the box. The boy stepped into the water, but Frog splashed away, spraying water all around.

Goat wondered about the splashing. Though he did not want to, Goat ran back to the lake. By then, the boy had already picked up Frog by the throat.

All at once, Goat ran into the lake. Cold water sprayed all over the boy. The boy was so surprised; he dropped Frog and ran away.

Frog was so scared that he shook all over. Finally, Frog said, "Thank you for saving me. If you had not come along, I would already be in the box. Take a drink to wet your throat any time you like. Just don't drink the whole lake." So Goat drank water while Frog slept in the sun.

How Hen and Vulture Became Enemies by Moses Kudian

There was a time when Hen and Vulture were friends. One day Hen went to Vulture to borrow a razor so as to shave her children. She said, "Oh, friend Vulture, lend me your razor so that I can go and shave my children. They have a lot of dirty hair."

Vulture accepted Hen's request. He quickly lent Hen a razor without charging a fee as he did with other borrowers. However, Vulture cautioned Hen to return it quickly. Hen thanked Vulture for his generosity. As the saying goes, "A friend in need is a friend indeed." Hen promised to return the razor without failure.

When she reached home, Hen shaved her children till they shone like moonlight. Then she put the razor in a certain leather bag in a corner of her house.

Days went by and Hen did not return Vulture's razor. So Vulture became impatient because it was the only razor he had. It was also the one that earned him a living. When he could no longer wait,

Vulture went to Hen's home to get his razor.

Hen said, "Oh, friend Vulture, forgive me for my carelessness. I wanted to bring your razor but I forgot where I kept it. Give me a little time to search."

Vulture, chocked with anger, said, "You! Look here, thankless Hen, see how you have punished me. How can you refuse to return my razor? You will pay for it dearly."

Hen flew inside the house and searched everywhere. She checked in the leather bag, but it was not there! She was stunned to find it missing.

After checking in every corner, Hen failed to find it. She knelt in front of Vulture asking to be given a few more days. Vulture agreed, but not without a warning. Said Vulture, "I told you to take good care of my razor. Remember that you must return the very razor I gave you. I won't accept another."

Hen continued with her frantic search. At last she had to demolish the house so as to check in the grass thatch. She checked in the ashes, in the sand, and in the rubbish pit, but it was all in vain.

The next day, Vulture returned to receive his property. He found Hen still searching. She was by then clawing in the grass and scattered rubbish. But no way! This time Vulture was not prepared to accept any excuse. He told Hen, "My friend Hen, I am sorry I cannot wait any more. From now on you will be giving me one chicken whenever I come, until you return my razor."

With those words, Vulture flew high in the sky, snatching one chick in his claws. That is why Hen is always scratching in the earth in search of Vulture's razor.

Ostrich and the Snake by Derrick

The friendship between Ostrich and Snake always amazed the other animals. The two were too close. They did many things together like looking for food, organizing parties in turns in their houses, and looking after their young ones.

Whenever one fell sick, the other animal would ensure all the children from both families were taken well care of. In fact, they seemed like one family. But Ostrich was also popular with other animals. They particularly liked Ostrich because of her beauty; the way she walked and carried herself. She laughed easily with other animals and would not hesitate to help them. Snake did not quite get along with others because he liked keeping to himself when not with Ostrich.

It was, however, not easy to break the friendship between Snake and Ostrich. Some animals had a very strong dislike for Snake. They often wondered what Ostrich saw in Snake to have him as a friend. Mouse especially did not like Snake because snakes kill and eat young mice.

I will spoil Snake's relationship with Ostrich, then Snake will have no one to cry to when he has problems, Mouse confided to his colleagues. It was not easy to break the friendship, though. Mouse watched the movements of Snake for a long time, waiting for his opportunity.

But due to Ostrich's popularity with the rest of the animals, Snake was uneasy. In fact, Snake was jealous of his friend. Snake tried talking to Ostrich about it, saying the other animals could ruin their relationship. "You should never show any interest in them. Even though they appear to like you and want to laugh with you, you may never know what their motives are," Snake cautioned.

"Ah ha, don't be funny my friend, these animals mean no ill at all. Besides, at the bottom of my heart, I always know you are the only true friend I have. There is no harm in chatting with them," Ostrich replied.

Snake was not happy with Ostrich's response. He decided he would poison her egg before it hatched to teach her a lesson. But unknown to Snake, his enemy, Mouse, was watching his movements. When Snake had finished poisoning Ostrich's egg, Mouse came out of his hiding place and shouted, "You little witch. I always knew you only pretended to be Ostrich's friend. I will tell her of your evil ways."

Snake was terrified, but before he could plead with Mouse not to say a word to Ostrich, Mouse was already disclosing the sad news.

"I am so disappointed with you, Snake. All along you pretended to be my friend. I will never trust you again," Ostrich said.

"But please, Mouse is telling lies. Do not listen," Snake stuttered. Ostrich cut him short. "I never want to be your friend again. You have betrayed my trust." The two became enemies. Other animals sympathized with Ostrich, while Snake became a loner.

The Animal Feast by Isabella Chebet

Once upon a time, there lived a squirrel and a buffalo. They were great friends, always working in partnership and spending most of their time together. Squirrel was a marvelous dancer while Buffalo was a wonderful singer, and they loved singing and dancing together.

Now one day there was to be a great feast to celebrate the harvest, but only animals with horns were invited, with only one exception, Lion. Lion was king, so he must come, but no one else without horns was allowed.

Buffalo had big horns, beautifully curved ones, as you know. So, he was all set to go and began practicing his songs for the occasion. But what about his favorite dancing partner? Squirrel had no horns, but Buffalo was determined to find a way to slip Squirrel into the party.

Squirrel was keen to attend, even though he knew he did not qualify and was not allowed. So, the two friends put their heads together to think about how to do it.

They came up with an amazing solution, which was to make horns for Squirrel and find a way to fix them onto his head. They visited the bees and were given beeswax to use for glue.

Sticks became sticky with glue, then fixed together into a very amazing horny headdress. All this was glued onto Squirrel's head, so that he almost looked as much a horned animal as any other.

The day of the feast arrived and the two friends showed up early for the occasion. As Buffalo took up his singing position in the front, he advised his friend Squirrel to stay behind the other animals and not to dance too vigorously this time.

Then the eating and singing and dancing began and all the animals joined in.

At first, Squirrel took his position in the back as agreed, while

Buffalo sat on the platform at the front to lead the singing. But with the great music, Squirrel could not resist the lively beat of the drum. He started dancing vigorously, shaking his head up and down, forgetting all about his friend's advice.

The other animals were so impressed by Squirrel's dancing skills

that they invited him to dance right up front, on top of the platform in the very center, so that all could see.

Squirrel was so flattered and so energized and alive with excitement that he lost all his good sense and accepted their invitation. Up front he went, dancing more wildly than ever as all the other animals clapped and cheered.

When he saw this, Buffalo was really worried about his friend's "horns", so he changed his tune to a slower rhythm and even put words in his song to warn Squirrel to go slower.

But Squirrel was so engrossed in the dancing that he did not pay attention to the words of his friend and right in the middle of the song, swinging his hips and shaking his head, the glue became unstuck and off fell Squirrel's "horns".

The other animals looked down at the pile of sticky sticks and up at Squirrel with shock and surprise.

The Leopard And The Hare by Diana

Hare had tricked Leopard several times so that Leopard was really mad at Hare. "When I catch Hare, I will squeeze him until he becomes mincemeat. I am going to teach him a lesson."

Leopard thought really hard and came up with a plan. He went to his bed and loosely covered himself with a thick blanket. He made himself still and stiff and pretended to be dead. He was sure Hare would come to look at his dead body just for the fun of it.

"When Hare comes to look at me," Leopard said to himself, "I will pounce on him."

As he lay there, Leopard called his wife, who came immediately. "My dear wife, I am now dead."

"Dead! What do you mean dead?" Mrs. Leopard asked.

"Well, I am not dead now, but I die as soon as I give these instructions."

"I still do not understand," said Mrs. Leopard.

"Let me explain then, and please promise to help me. I want to get Hare and finish his mean tricks. Go to the yard and shout as loudly as you can. Announce to the neighbors that I am dead, very dead."

Mrs. Leopard went outside and let a wail that shook the whole neighborhood. In fact, she wailed so much that the neighbors thought that perhaps the whole village was on fire. Within no time, Leopard's compound was full of concerned neighbors. They were all sad, worried and full of sympathy for Mrs. Leopard. Mrs. Leopard was crying herself out. "My husband is dead! Oh, Leopard is no more," she wailed.

Hare could hear the mournful shouts in his house, some distance away. But he asked himself, "How come Leopard has died? I have not heard a thing about his illness. Leopard is so strong and well fed. How does he just die all of a sudden?"

Hare found himself among the crowd in Leopard's compound. He asked Monkey, "My brother, did you ever hear that Leopard was sick?"

"No, I never heard it at all," replied Monkey.

Hare went to Goat. "Goat, did you hear that Leopard was sick?"

"No, I never heard," Goat said.

"Did anyone try to take Leopard to hospital?" asked Hare.

At this point, Mrs. Leopard, who had not stopped crying, answered, "Death came upon him without warning; struck at once! It would have been useless to take him to hospital."

"I see," answered Hare. Hare, together with the rest of the crowd, stood at the door. Then Hare addressed Mrs. Leopard.

"Did Leopard shake and cry out before he died?"

When Leopard heard Hare's words, he shook himself and cried out as loudly as he could. Hare burst out laughing. "Wonder of wonders! Since when did the dead shake and howl?" Everybody could tell that Leopard was just pretending to be dead.

Leopard, too, was confused. His trick had failed miserably but he was not going to let this chance slip by. He sprung from his bed and jumped after Hare. Hare reacted very quickly and ran away. Mrs. Leopard, embarrassed, ran and hid in a bush behind the house.

All the other animals were angry at Leopard. They decided to hold a meeting to discuss how they could teach Leopard a lesson he wouldn't forget.

The Wise Old Man by Sylvia Cheptoo

Once there was a poor old man named Andrew who lived in a small hut in the village. After the death of his wife, he was alone, as he had no children.

But Andrew was still healthy and strong. He was always busy helping his neighbors in one way or another and in return, they gave him food. As he was polite and humble, everybody liked him and nobody refused him anything.

He liked children very much and whenever he was free he would tell stories to the children. So, he was very popular among the children and they addressed him as "Baba".

One day, when he was sitting alone in his hut, he started thinking, "Day by day, I am getting older and older and within a short time, I shall die. After the death of my wife, the people gave me free food."

After some time, Andrew nodded his head with a smile. He started murmuring, "It is wonderful! It is wonderful! I must do it."

The following day, he said to all the children, "Whenever you eat any fruits, please do not throw away the seeds but bring them to me." Within a few days, the children had brought him seeds of mango, pawpaw, orange, plum, peach, lemon, and many more fruits.

After drying the seeds in sunshine for a few weeks, he planted all these seeds near his hut and asked the children to help him in making a fence around so that the seeds could not be spoiled by anybody.

Every day he watered them. Within a few days the soil was covered with small seedlings of different fruit. Then he waited for the long rains.

On arrival of long rains, he became very happy and started planting the seedlings at a distance of about two hundred meters on both sides of a road leading into a town.

On seeing him do this, the children helped him, planting and fencing the seedlings. The children helped the work of planting the seedlings on the whole road. For one year, he looked after these plants properly.

After two or three rainy seasons, people were happy to see different types of fruit trees growing on both sides of the road. After a few years, the trees were covered with fruit. But, there was no Andrew to see the fruit on the trees.

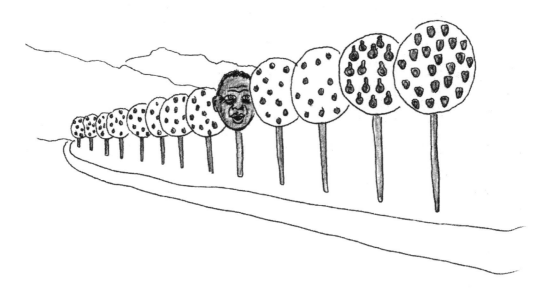

Everyone, young and old, rich and poor, who traveled on the road stopped to take a rest under the shade of the trees and to eat some of the fruit. While eating these fruits, they praised Andrew for his noble work. Andrew was no more, but the trees were there to tell the travellers about the work of Andrew. In this way, Andrew became immortal.

Do Your Part

There is no room for selfishness in the village. We work together. One person collects water for the village, other's take care of the camels, some is scouting for fresh grass in the next valley. But if one person isn't willing to help, than the whole village suffers.

Greedy Hyena by Isabella Chebet

Once upon a time, long ago, in a certain valley called Thikio, lived a peaceful community of animals and people. They were all great friends, always ready to help each other when the need arose.

Among the young people in the community was a very beautiful girl who had reached the age of marriage. She became engaged to a handsome young man from the opposite side of the valley and everyone was looking forward to their wedding.

Her parents, though, were poor; so poor they couldn't afford to feed the many guests they knew would come during the lengthy wedding process.

"Oh, Oh," the two parents cried. "Now what are we going to do?" It was not until the rest of the community came to learn that the girl's parents had little to offer that they understood why the wedding celebrations were taking so long to organize.

"Hey! Don't worry," everyone said to the parents of the girl. "We'll help!"

"I will give a bull to be slaughtered," shouted the chief. "I'll give a bag of rice," shouted another. At last, the wedding process could move ahead, and a date was set for the big feast in the girl's village to welcome the boy's family. Everybody made a pledge to help and contribute; everybody except Hyena.

When Hyena heard the news, he went home rejoicing. "Hoh, a day is coming when I'll eat and eat without working," he thought to himself.

And, indeed, in the days thereafter, he avoided all the planning meetings and never made any effort to contribute. As a result, when the big party day arrived, he had no idea of the arrangements.

The community plan was to cook on each side of the valley and then bring all the dishes together to the special place they had decided for the party. On the set day, everyone was busy and by afternoon, the smell of good food floated out from both sides of the valley.

Meanwhile, Hyena was just sleeping until a fly tickled him awake. "Umps, what's the time," cried Hyena? "Am I already late?" He dashed out, jogging up and down, as hyenas do, towards where he thought the big party was going to be.

On his way, Hyena reached a fork in the road where the forest path divided off to the right and to the left. "Ah, ah," Hyena could smell roasted meat from both directions and his mouth just watered.

"Mmm! Oh my!" Off to the right side was the sweet smell of chicken biryani and over on the left was the irresistible smell of chapattis and sweet potatoes in peanut sauce. "Sniff, sniff." He stepped to the right one foot, to the left one foot. So much wonderful aroma of food, it just drove him crazy. Hyena was greedy and Hyena wanted it all. So he tried to move towards the food on both sides at once. One foot to the right; one foot to the left. Further to the right and f-u-r-t-h-e-r to the left. A little more to the right; a little more to the left.

It was quite a big stretch, but Hyena tried to move each foot in

opposite directions at the same time towards all those delicious foods until, all of a sudden, POP! He just split into two. Poor Hyena. It was his end.

Hare and Hyena by Joy Relin

A long time ago, Hare and Hyena were friends. They lived near the Nyando River. The two spent most of their time fishing.

One day, however, during the rainy season, there were heavy floods. The river was so flooded that their boat capsized and it was completely destroyed. The two could not fish any more. Food was very expensive and they could not afford to buy it.

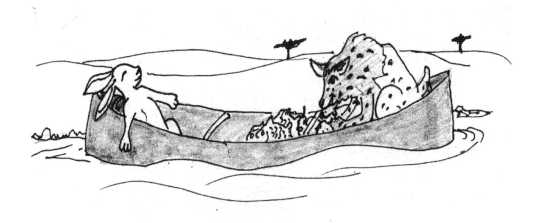

The two went to the market and bought a large cassava. They were to make it into a boat. Hyena was very cunning. He wanted to dig out the cassava all by himself. He therefore asked the Hare to fetch firewood. Hyena ate all the cassava pieces since he was very hungry. The inside of the boat was very thin.

On coming back, Hare was disappointed to see that the walls of the boat were so thin. But Hyena told him the thinner the walls of the canoe the better. It is lighter and will float better.

The two friends decided to go fishing since the water was now calm. Hare was able to catch a number of fish. It was now the turn of

Hyena since Hare was tired. As Hyena struggled to catch the fish, Hare feel asleep. Hyena felt really hungry and decided to taste the fish. He ate one after the other until all of them were gone. Hyena did not feel satisfied, so he started eating the walls of the boat. After eating so much, water entered the boat and the boat began to sink. Hyena was very scared and he swam away without alerting the Hare, who was still asleep.

The cold water woke the Hare. He almost drowned but struggled to get back to the riverbank. The two animals became enemies and Hare still looks for revenge against Hyena.

The Dishonest Crow by Kelvin Mnang'at

A long time ago, a family of crows lived and collected fruit together. At dawn, they would fly to distant fields and come back at dusk with different kinds of fruits. They ate the ripe ones and kept fruits that were unripe for future use, especially on weekends when they usually rested.

The crows would dig small holes in their garden, where they stored the green fruits to ripen. Because they trusted each other, the birds

worked under their chief. One day, Tumbo Kubwo, a member of the family, excused himself from going to the fields. "I am not feeling well today," he pleaded. When you come back, remember to bring me some fruits.

Other crows sympathized with him and left for the fields. Immediately after he was left on his own, he laughed, saying, "There is no need of travelling long distance in search of fruits when I can eat what is in the store." With that, he ate some of the fruits that had been buried to ripen. When the others came back in the evening, they found him lying on the ground complaining of a stomachache.

Sympathetic, they consoled him and offered him some of the fruits. He ate little, citing his ill health.

The following day, the same thing happened. This time, he hid some of the fruits. When other crows came back, they found him vomiting. Surprisingly, what he vomited was much more than he had eaten the previous night.

After six days, the chief said it was time to take a rest and eat what had been collected for the last six days. The chief ordered some of the stronger crows to bring the stored fruits. Going to their holes, the birds did not find any fruit. "It is sad to tell you, but the fruits we have been keeping are not there." The chief and the others could not believe their ears and went to confirm for themselves.

They asked each other if anyone had seen a thief, but they all said they had not. Tumbo Kubwo also said he hadn't seen anyone stealing. "I am not the one who ate the fruits," he said.

The chief said he knew how to catch the thief. He sent for a rope and ordered that it be tied to two tall trees. Under the rope was a river. The chief ordered that each crow had to recite some words before jumping over the rope. Any crow who would fail the test would be the thief and be punished. All the crows passed but Tumbo Kubwo, who, too fat from eating all week, fell into the river. He cried for help as the river carried him away, but no one helped him.

The Elephant and the Hare by Sharon

Once upon a time, a hare and an elephant became great friends. They always went around together. One day, they bought some land from a rhino, who had lost all his money. Elephant and Hare made up their minds to cultivate it together.

"We won't divide it into two parts," they said, "because then other animals will think we aren't friends any more."

The day came when the friends decided to start digging the land. Hare arrived dressed in leopard and cobra skin with a necklace of brightly colored beads.

"Why are you dressed like that?" asked Elephant, who was very angry. "This is not a day for dancing. We've agreed to work today."

"I'm sorry," replied Hare, "but I can't possibly work in these clothes."

Elephant was very angry and divided the land into two halves. He began to till his piece. Helped by his hunger, he worked very fast.

"Everyone will laugh at you," said Hare. "They will wonder why such a big animal as you is leaving the same amount of work for a tiny animal like me."

Elephant felt ashamed! He changed his mind and at once started to dig Hare's portion of the land.

Hare was very pleased and made some strong sugarcane honey beer to show his thanks. Then heavy rains fell and Elephant and his relatives planted the land with sweet potatoes. The crop grew so well that the potatoes looked like huge rocks.

After a while, Elephant found that as soon as the potatoes appeared, they disappeared. He suspected that Hare was the thief.

So, elephant dug three very deep holes near a large group of potatoes sticking out of the earth. Then he put sticks across the top of the holes and earth over the sticks, so that no one could see the trap.

On the next day, Hare went to dig up some potatoes for his evening meal, as he did every day. "Why don't I take my share? After all, I paid as much for the land as Elephant."

When he got near the field, he saw all the big, ripe potatoes. He ran to them, but there was a horrid sound. Then, "Hwaa!," Hare cried as he sank into the ground. He cried and cried for help, but no one came. After a while, he stopped jumbling about and lay still. What else could he do?

About an hour later, Elephant came. He was pleased to see that Hare was trapped. He put his trunk into the hole and pulled up the thief, shook him and threw him to the ground. Hare lay still and elephant thought Hare was dead.

He left Hare and went home. Elephant proudly told his relatives how he had killed the potato thief. Then he brewed some beer and made a great feast for his relatives.

That evening, a cool wind blew over dying Hare so that he was able to walk slowly out from the trap to his home. Some of his bones were broken and clicked. He called Squirrel, the village doctor, who gave him all kinds of treatment. After many days, Hare was well enough to walk about.

When Elephant heard that Hare was alive, he could hardly believe it. However, one evening there was a dance called "cha-cha" near Hare's home. Both Hare and Elephant went to the dance.

When the dance began, all the ladies wanted to dance with Hare. Hare's bones had never healed properly and when he moved, they still clicked and clacked. The ladies thought he made the noise to add to the rhythm of the dance.

Elephant could only wobble around and was very clumsy. No one wanted to dance with him. He was so upset he went home.

The next day, Elephant decided to visit Hare. He wanted to make friends with him again, but he especially wanted to know how he could make his bones click as he danced so that he could attract girls. Elephant felt ashamed that none of the ladies had wanted to dance with him, even though he was a much bigger creature than Hare.

Hare told him to come back the next day. By then, Hare could have a plan ready. Elephant agreed. When Elephant returned the following morning, Hare told him to lie down. Then Hare cut open Elephant's stomach with axes, hoes, and sharp knives. It was very painful.

"I can't bear it any more. Let me go!" screamed Elephant.

"You must bear it a little more if you want to be beautiful," replied Hare.

Then Hare threw the axes, hoes and sharp knives into elephant's stomach, and added a few sharp stones before he sewed Elephant back up.

"You'll be a star at the next dance. All the ladies will want you," Hare said to Elephant.

The Hare and the Hyena Herd Cows by Kelvin Mnang'at

A long time age, there lived a hare and a hyena. The two animals were friends. Their friendship was so strong that nobody could separate them. They did almost everything at the same time, always helping each other.

One season, there was drought and there was not enough food for the two animals. They were so hungry that they were forced to go to the forest long miles away. The two animals walked as slowly as a tortoise because they had empty stomachs. They did not have enough energy and they were very thirsty.

It took them two hours to reach the forest. They were relieved because they saw ripened fruits. They quickly picked the fruits and ate them. A short distance away, they saw a lot of cows without a shepherd. Wow! They did not believe their eyes. They hurried to the cows and drove them away.

They started their journey back home, driving the cows before them. This time, they walked quickly and arrived within an hour. Hare and Hyena were happy since now they knew they would not die from hunger. They slaughtered one big bull and roasted the meat. They ate happily as they divided the duties for looking after the cows.

First, it was Hyena's turn. He woke to graze the cows very early in the morning. Later in the evening, he came back home very happy.

Hare quickly counted the cows and noticed one was missing. "Where is our red cow?" Hyena simply nodded his head, saying nothing. Hare was very unhappy about that.

The next day, it was Hare's turn. He drove off the cows early in the morning as Hyena did. Later in the evening, Hare brought the cows back home and counted them. They were all there. Hare was happy with his good job of taking care of the cows.

The next day, it was Hyena's turn. He drove the animals in the morning as usual. Later in the evening, Hyena brought the cows back home. Hare counted them and found one was missing. He asked, but Hyena just nodded his head. Hare was now very unhappy about what Hyena was doing.

That night, Hare did not sleep. He was thinking of a plan that he would use to challenge Hyena's plan. "I have an idea," Hare said to himself. The next morning, Hare drove the animals as usual to graze. This time, he carried a sharp knife with him.

While at the grazing field, Hare quickly chopped off all the cow's tails and planted them in the ground, the end of the tail sticking out. He drove all the cows to his grandmother's home.

Then Hare returned to the grazing field and screamed. Hyena came quickly. "Our cows are sinking!" screamed Hare.

Hyena tried to pull them out but only the tails came out. Hyena burst into a loud cry. Hare also pretended to cry. They walked home very slowly and Hare knew his plan was working. Hyena did not stop crying. Tears flowed down his tomato-like cheeks like water forming a wonderful number eleven.

Hare, satisfied with himself, went to live with his grandmother. Hyena was left, dying of hunger. Tit for tat is a fair game.

The Hare and the Lion by Isabella Chebet

One day, Lion was moving through the jungle looking for food, but all in vain. He was unlucky and found nothing to eat that day. As he walked along, he became weaker and weaker.

As Lion staggered along, hungry and weak, he saw a tree with big branches that made a cool shade. As he prepared to lie down, Hare happened to pass by. Hare was quite astonished and shocked to see Lion looking so weak and tired.

He asked Lion, "What is wrong?"

Not wanting to admit that he had failed in the hunt that day, and looking for an easy way to get a meal, Lion pretended to be quite well, except for his back foot.

"Hoh, friend Hare," Lion explained, "as I walked through the jungle this morning, I must have stepped on a thorny stick. A big, sharp thorn has gone right through my back foot and it's so painful that I couldn't walk any more. Please, please, come over and remove it for me."

When Hare moved closer to do the needful, Lion took advantage of the situation and grabbed Hare by his leg.

"Ah, hah! Just what I have been waiting for!" roared Lion. I have been struggling the whole day to find some food without success. Now at last, God has granted my prayer. I am going to eat you."

Hare was quite shaken, but had a lot of courage and knew how to use his head.

"Oh, my friend," Hare said. "Why didn't you tell me you were hungry? I am very small and pretty thin these days. I could never satisfy you. But I know where there is lots of food and tasty, too. Just let go of me so I can lead you to where I saw some nice fat antelope sleeping in the bush."

"Fat antelope?" Lion became so interested in this plan that he asked Hare to show him the way. As they moved forward together, Hare went a little faster, and a little faster, and a little f-a-s-t-e-r.

Hare burst into full speed with as much strength as he had and disappeared into the bush, never to be seen again, leaving Lion stranded and still hungry.

The Poor Man by Levi Pkiach

Once there was a poor man who lived with his wife in a town. Their neighbors were very rich, but the couple was poor. The man and his wife wished they could be as rich as their neighbors, but they weren't.

One day, a fairy came and promised to give them four wishes. They could wish for anything they wanted and their wish would be granted. The man and his wife wished to be wealthy, healthy, and have long life. But they could not agree on who would make the wish and what the exact wish would be. Days passed while they thought about this.

Then one day, as they were about to have tea, the wife said, "I wish we had some bread." Instantly, there was bread in her hands.

The man was very angry that his wife had wasted a wish. In his anger, he shouted, "I wish the bread got into your nose instead of your mouth." Immediately, the bread stuck in the wife's nose. It was very uncomfortable and she couldn't breathe.

"How I wish the bread could fall off my nose," the wife said angrily. Immediately, the bread left the wife's nose and the two realized what had just happened. The two stopped talking to each other.

A few days later, the man went to steal some egg from his neighbor's compound. He returned home and went straight to the kitchen. Before he could cook the eggs, he heard footsteps. He put the egg on the seat and quickly sat on it. Suddenly, there was a horrible smell. The egg was rotten and it broke! Within no time, the room was filled with flies. His wife's angry stare told him what happened.

Do's and Don'ts

Villages can be a dangerous place to grow up. With Lions and hyena's roaming the hills and warriors from the next tribe looking to steal a young herd's boy's cows. The rules are like the thorn fences around our huts. They are there to keep us safe, but will hurt anyone who tries to cross them without permission.

Ndogo, the Springhare by Nathan Pkemoi

(a Springhare hops like a kangaroo. Ndogo is Swahili for "small")

Once there was a small springhare with beautiful black and white fur. His name was Ndogo. He lived with his friends in a place with many grasshoppers and other small animals.

"I am a strong and powerful springhare. Am I not, my friend?" Ndogo stated.

"Yes, you are, friend, but remember you are our friend and only a springhare."

When walking in the bush, Ndogo would come upon birds or grasshoppers or ants or spiders and he would scare them away. When he saw a butterfly, he would run towards it and scare it away. "I am a strong and powerful springhare," Ndogo yelled.

Sometimes he beat small creatures with his hands. Sometimes he would chase small creatures and kick them or flick them with his tail. He would come back in the evening and say to his friends, "I am a strong, powerful, and irresistible springhare."

"You are the strongest," his friends would say, "but remember you are our friend, and you are only a springhare."

Some days, he would sneak up on his friends and scare them and chase them away. "Ha, ha, ha! I am the strongest," he would boast.

One evening, rain started and with it the wind blew very hard. All his friends were afraid as the trees shook. Ndogo ran outside and shouted at the wind and the rain. He whipped the rain with his tail and kicked the wind with his legs. He even hit the wind with his head and the rain and the wind stopped. "See, I am the strongest and most powerful. I am more powerful than the wind and the rain. I chased them away."

He felt so proud of himself. The next day Ndogo decided he would walk until he found something really big to scare. No more grasshoppers and butterflies. He could now scare even wind and rain. He needed something even bigger to scare.

He walked and walked until he came to a big hill. "I will scare that big hill." Ndogo shouted at the hill, "Go away!" But the hill just stood there, doing nothing.

Ndogo then hit the hill with his feet. He even hit the hill with his head. He shouted, "Run out of my way." But the hill was still there, not moving.

It was getting late and the sun was setting in the west. Ndogo decided to go home and rest. As he walked away, he looked back at the hill as it stood under the setting sun and said, "You big hill, I will come back tomorrow and knock you down."

The next day, he went out searching for the big hill but couldn't remember where it was. All he could remember was that it was under the sun. Ndogo walked and walked, but he couldn't find the hill. "Now I know what happened," he said to himself. "The hill has run away. I scared it away. Ha, ha, ha! I am the most powerful springhare in the world." He danced and sang happily for having scared away the hill.

Ndogo went on walking. He now felt so important that he changed his walking style. He kept swinging his hips. As he walked he saw a lot of water. Ndogo had never seen so much water. The water went on forever.

"Go away," Ndogo said to the water. Waves of water just kept washing up on the shore. "I want to pass. I am the strongest springhare and I command you to go away," Ndogo said to the water. Waves of water just kept washing up on the shore.

Ndogo kicked the water with his feet. Ndogo struck the water with his tail. Ndogo hit the water with his head. The water didn't seem to notice. Waves just kept washing up on the shore.

Ndogo was now very tired, so he laid down and fell asleep. When he awoke, the water was a long way out. "Yes!" Ndogo exclaimed. "I chased the water away. I am so powerful even the water listens." He was very pleased with himself.

A week later, Ndogo wanted to go out walking again. A friend said, "I will walk with you."

After walking for a while, the friend noticed branches moving and then felt a breeze on his face. "What is that?" the friend asked. "Oh, that is the wind," Ndogo said. "I scared it away once. Now I am angry it has come back."

Then they noticed they could see a long way. The friend said, "I think we are on a hill." Ndogo was very angry that the hill had come back. Then the friend looked out from the hill and saw water, as far as he could see. "Is that the sea?" the friend asked. Ndogo said, "It can't be. I chased it away." The friend said, "Remember, Ndogo, even though you are very powerful, there are some things springhares just can't do."

Ngura The Ogre by Titus Kiptoo

The people of the fertile plains of Kukdin in Pokot land held a big ceremony dance. It was the festival dance that marked every bountiful season of harvest. Many people came to this dance decorated and adorned in beautiful clothes. Many young men were dressed in ravishing clothes. One of them seemed to be the most handsome and attractive.

His attractiveness coupled with his superior dancing style made all the girls long to dance with him. When the dance was over, many girls followed this handsome young man to his home. They walked and walked, talking little to each other except whispering here and there. The young man strode on, the girls talking behind him. Then he stopped and broke the silence.

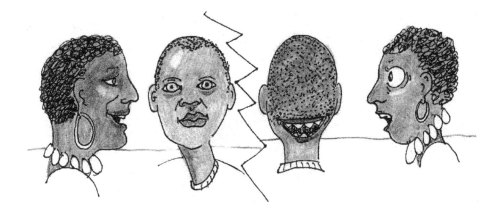

"Gi rls of the plain, my name is Ngura. Having admired your great company, I now request the pleasure of you to accompany me to my place." They continued to walk in silence. Suddenly, Ngura jumped and the hair at the back of his head rose up. "There!" Some of the girls saw the mouth that was hidden at the back of his head. This realization gave them cold chills down their spines.

One of the girls whispered in horror, "Ho! This is not a man but an ogre. Let me go back and warn my friends."

As the party neared the edge of the forest, Ngura told them, "Now we are very near my home. I will leave you a little while. I have to hurry because I hear a lamb crying. I must hurry to release it so it can get milk with its mother."

By now the girls were alarmed, so they all rushed off and went to collect armed villagers with spears and bows. When they returned to his house, he was eating a large bone. Warriors killed him and the villagers were happy.

The Hare And The Elephant by Derrick

One day Kaka Sungura, the hare, sat on the bank of a river wondering how he could pass across the river with fast moving water. Fortunately, as he sat contemplating, a herd of elephants came along. He approached them and asked, "Where are you great gentlemen going today?"

The largest elephant came forward and replied, "We are going to take this gift of honey to my father-in-law, who lives across the river." He proudly held up the leather bag of honey he was carrying.

"Would you please give your poor little friend a ride across the river?" asked Kaka, shyly.

"Gladly," said Elephant, giving him the bag of honey to hold and lifting Kaka up with his trunk onto his back. They started crossing the dangerous river. Meanwhile, Kaka decided this is an opportunity he could not afford to pass. He drank all the honey. Unfortunately, some of the honey fell from his long whiskers onto the elephant's broad back.

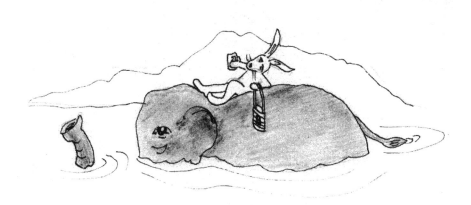

"What is that dropping on my back?" Elephant asked as they approached the other side of the river. "The tear of your little friend", replied Kaka. "I am crying because I am so grateful to you for help." As they reached the other side of the river, Kaka asked Elephant to pass him some stones, which he said he wanted to throw at the noisy birds in a nearby tree. Kaka put the stones into the honey bag and returned it to its owner and asked to be lowered to the ground.

When Kaka was safely down, he ran away and hid in a nearby hole in the ground. Meanwhile, Elephant soon discovered the trick and ran after him. Elephant put his great trunk down the hole and seized Kaka by a leg. Kaka laughed and called out, "You have got hold of a root! You have got hold of a root!" Elephant immediately let go and felt around in the hole until his trunk found a strong big root. Kaka cried out, "Oh! You are breaking my leg! You are breaking my leg!" Kaka screamed as loud as he could. The angry elephant pulled very hard and soon he fell back. Then Kaka ran out of the hole and escaped into the bush where some baboons were living.

Elephant chased the hare again. As he approached, Kaka begged the baboons not to say where he was and they agreed. Elephant asked the baboons, "Have you seen the hare who stole my honey?"

"Oh, yes," they replied, "and we know where he is hiding."

"Do tell me, then," implored Elephant.

"We will, we will," shouted the baboons from the tree, "but we expect you to give us something in return."

"What is it and I will give it to you," said Elephant.

"What we ask is that you give us a small cupful of your blood," they said as one of them held a small cup for him to see.

"Oh, that is a simple thing. Here make a hole in my skin and draw your cup of blood and then tell me where the hare is hiding."

The baboon made a hole in Elephant's thick skin and let the blood run into the cup. After a few seconds elapsed, Elephant turned to see if the cup was full, and started to lose his patience. When the baboons realized he was impatient, they said to him, "A great animal like you should not be troubled about a small drop of blood."

"Oh, no! Not at all", said Elephant, reluctant to admit it was painful, lest the baboons think him weak.

However, Elephant did not know that the cup had a hole in the bottom. In a little while, he collapsed and died from loss of blood. Kaka came out of hiding grinning, as he was now safe.

Hare, Hyena, and Dog by Moses Kudian

Long ago Hare, Hyena, and Dog lived as great friends. Even other animals would always shudder with amazement how these three animals could be so friendly and yet very different from each other.

Then one day, Hyena's in-laws invited him to a party. Like a good friend, Hyena decided to ask his friends to accompany him to the feast. The friends on their part did not disappoint him and they agreed to join him.

Hyena and his friends were given reception on the highest degree one could expect from the in-laws. They were taken to a great feast. They ate and drank to their fill. They danced and got the best possible entertainment. It was really an entertaining visit; a very colorful entertainment!

After dark, Hyena and his friends were shown where to sleep. This was in the same room where sheep and goats were kept. But greedy Hyena could not be trusted. In the thick of the night, all the animals were deeply asleep except Hyena. Greedy Hyena could not control his hunger. He kept yawning and swallowing the saliva of a glutton and glancing at the sheep near him. He stealthily walked to one ram and held it by the throat so as not to make noise and awaken the friends.

Very quietly, Hyena strangled and ate the ram. Then he smeared red blood on the lips of his friends carefully and then went to sleep as if nothing had happened. But Hyena's trick did not quite work. His friends licked their lips while still in sleep and they became as clean as they had been before.

When Hyena's father in-law went to check his flock, he discovered that one ram was missing. He at once asked his guests to explain who was responsible for the ungrateful act. Nobody answered. Perhaps the matter would have ended there, unresolved. But Hare thought it was a good chance for him to track down the thief. So he called Hyena's father in-law and whispered for a little while. Then the father in-law left. No sooner had he left than he returned brandishing a panga (African tool like a machete) in hand and shouting viciously. "I have discovered the thief who killed my ram and I am going to teach him a lesson. I will slash and crush him like flour."

Hyena was already trembling with fear and trying hard not to show it. He was panic-stricken. Then suddenly, Dog dashed out and ran as fast as his legs could carry him with thin sweat dripping out his body. Hyena burst out into a loud laughter, which reached Dog's ears. This laughter made Dog confirm his fears that Hare actually blamed him for the offence. That is why to this day, Dog and Hare do not see eye to eye.

The Lion and The Leopard by Silas Yego

A long time ago, Lion and Leopard were friends. They were always hunting together. However, Lion was slower than Leopard when it came to preying and killing other animals for food. Lion's role was to skin the animal since his claws were sharper, so they shared the hunt equally.

Then the unexpected happened. There was a great famine and the animals migrated to greener pasture. For Leopard and Lion, there was nothing to eat. They slept on hungry stomachs for many nights. Then one day as Leopard was walking in the forest, he saw a young gazelle and he started running after it. Leopard pounced on it.

When the turn came for Lion to skin the gazelle, Leopard realized that large chunks of meat were peeled off as well as the skin. Lion ate everything and there was nothing left for Leopard. When Leopard asked Lion why he had eaten all the meat alone, Lion apologized saying the meat was too tender and it had stuck to his long claws, so he had to pull it out.

Then Lion started making promises that when they got more meat, he would leave it all to Leopard. But Leopard was so angry that he listened no more. He started walking back home slowly. Lion tracked closely behind. But luck was on Leopard's side as a hare crossed his path. He quickly pounced on it.

He would not share it with Lion however much Lion pleaded. Leopard started skinning the hare himself and sure enough his claws, too, could do the task. Lion started roaring in anger but to no avail as Leopard ran as fast as he could. Leopard then jumped up a tree and made himself comfortable and started eating. Lion attempted to climb up after Leopard, but in vain because Lion was heavier. Lion waited impatiently for Leopard to come down, but Leopard had eaten his fill and slept there peacefully. No wonder Leopard fancies staying in trees while Lion waits for him on the ground.

The Proud Ostrich by Sharon

Long ago there was a great famine in the land. There was not a drop of rain for many months. Day after day the sun shone and there was not a cloud in the sky. There were a few crops on the banks of tiny streams, but the rest of the land was dry and bare. Fires spread far and wide and there were many dust storms. Birds could not sing any longer as they were so hungry. The wild animals thought they would all die unless rain fell in the next few days.

But day after day the sky was clear. Water was so scarce that the lions even began to drink the morning dew from the grass. The hyenas and jackals also drank the dew, as did the moles and the fox. They prayed that someday soon there would be enough for all to drink. However, it appeared as if their prayers would not be answered.

The animals decided to have a meeting to see if they could think of a way to save their lives. The ostrich joined in, as well. It was agreed that he was more like an animal than a bird.

All the animals joined in except those who were sick. There were all kinds, big and small, young and old, flesh-eaters and grass-eaters. It was sad to see them so unhappy and sickly. They were all as thin as pieces of thread.

When Lion, their king, arrived, they all stood up. "Without water, we shall die," they cried.

"We have come to this place to talk about a very important matter. It is a matter of life or death," said Lion. "I suggest we dig a deep well near the fig tree across the Kagare Valley. Perhaps we can find enough water there to wet our tongues. The sooner we start, the better. There is no time to waste."

For a time, no one spoke, not even the brave leopard or the cheeky hare. Only the aged tortoise said, quietly, that Lion's idea was very wise.

The moles, the anteaters, and the other small creatures were frightened when they thought how deep the hole would need to be before they could reach water. But no one could think of a better idea. Lion decided they should all start to dig the well the next day. Once Lion makes a decision, it is final!

At dawn, Giraffe blew the horn very loudly, so no one could say he had not heard it. Jackals, hyena, moles, anteaters, tortoise, rats, ostrich, zebra, and many other animals arrived. They all came with spades and shovels and started to work. Though they were all very weak because they had had neither food nor water for so long, they worked as hard as they could. They wanted to finish the well in one day.

Suddenly, Hare noticed that Ostrich was not working. Instead, Ostrich flapped his wings about in a proud way. This made the other animals very cross.

"You take the shovel, next," Hare said to Ostrich.

"I can't dirty my pretty feathers," said Ostrich. "I can't get all muddy. I came here to wait until the other animals found water for me to drink."

When the other animals heard this, they chased Ostrich away.

"I don't want to drink your muddy water," said Ostrich. "I shall fly far away to a country where the rains never fail."

Digging the well was hard and dangerous. Five rats, one gorilla, three moles and two tortoises died while they were working. But finally, they reached water.

All the animals jumped up and down and danced when they saw the water. They were mad with joy. They all drank and some washed themselves, while ducks swam about happily.

"We'll guard the well," Lion said. "We won't let lazy Ostrich drink our water."

One day, Hippopotamus was on guard duty at the well when Ostrich came along, singing merrily;

"Water, water, but not for me,
    Ostrich, Ostrich is not to be
    Hi-ho-hi-ho-hoo;
    Hi-ho-hi-ho-hoo."

"You can't have even a sip of water from the well," said Hippo. "You refused to join us in digging the well."

"Please don't think I didn't want to work," said Ostrich. "I just don't want to make my beautiful feathers dirty. You should always be proud to see me with clean feathers. If you were a bird like me, you would know how good it is to be clean. I am not really an animal like you."

Hippo was very kind, and when Ostrich gave him some feathers, he said Ostrich could drink as much water as he liked.

When Ostrich had drunk his fill, he went away singing;

"Ostrich did not raise a toe,
   Ostrich has his stomach full,
   Yap, yap, yap;
   Yap, yap, yap."

The next day, Ostrich came again to the well to drink some water. As he came near the well, he sang;

"Water, water, but not for me,
    Ostrich, Ostrich is not to be
    Hi-ho-hi-ho-hoo;
    Hi-ho-hi-ho-hoo."

But this time, Donkey was on duty and not Hippo. Donkey was very angry when he heard Ostrich and was not going to let him drink water from the well.

Just as Ostrich bent down to drink, Donkey gave him a hard kick. Ostrich ran away and has not been seen since.

Pongio, The Snake Keeper by Boaz Kiptoo

Mary was a very old witch who was well known all over Toma village for her evil deeds. She was feared all over the place and mere mention of her name would attract evil spirits upon anyone. All of her neighbors were afraid of her and never mentioned her name or gossiped about her. Mary was known for keeping snakes and people who heard her story for the first time couldn't believe it. No one could imagine how a woman could ever stay close to snakes.

Mary kept a very big venomous snake in her house. It was very large and whenever anyone called Mary by her name, the snake appeared from nowhere. If you were unfortunate, it could kill you.

Parents warned their children against calling her name and no newborn babies were named after her. The whole village nicknamed her "Pongio", to mean the evil woman. Parents made sure their children were not aware of her real name. Children were told to call her

Pongio. This was the only safe name.

One evening, Mary happened to pass by fellow villagers having a community party. She was not aware of the party and had not been invited. She decided to go to the party anyway.

One furious man, Okudo, whose son had been killed by Mary's snake, sprang up and shouted her real name, "Mary". Instantly, the snake appeared in front of Okudo, ready to strike and kill him. People tried to kill the snake with spears and swords, but the snake got away.

The villagers made a plan to get rid of this evil forever. They decided to make torches and burn her house. From that day, the village people were happy because Mary and all her snakes were gone.

The Tortoise and the Lizard by Abigael Cherop

Once upon a time, the tortoise and the lizard were neighbors. Tortoise lived in the deep grass and Lizard lived in a small hole under the ground.

One day, Lizard was peeping out of his hole when he saw Tortoise walking to the market. Tortoise was dragging along a bag of salt to sell. The bag was tied to a cord around his neck.

As quick as lightening, Lizard shot down into his hole and came up with a sharp knife. He cut the cord holding the bag of salt and dragged the bag down into his underground home.

Imagine Tortoise's dismay when he reached the market and found no salt on the end of the cord! Miserably, Tortoise walked home. Seeing Lizard basking in the sun, he asked, "Did you see a bag of salt on the road?"

"No," replied Lizard, "But I did see a bag of salt walking along all by itself. I invited it to stay in my hole."

Angrily, Tortoise went home. Next time when he passed by, he saw Lizard's head inside the hole, and his tail sticking out. Taking out his pocketknife, Tortoise cut off lizard's tail and he went away. Lizard felt a sharp pain so he came out of his hole to see what happened. He couldn't believe his eyes. His tail was not there. He only saw the stump where his tail had been.

"Friend Tortoise," he called out, "Have you seen my tail?"

"There was a tail lying in the sun, outside your hole, when I passed by," replied the smiling Tortoise. "I invited it to stay in my grassy home." Lizard was very annoyed but realized Tortoise was just as clever as he.

Growing Up

When you grow up, you become a leader in your community. It is now your turn to teach the children, find food, and protect the elders. To use your skills to help the village. This might mean getting a job at the bank or protecting the cows from a lion. But whatever you do, uphold the values the elders passed down to you.

Millie, the Pimbi, Likes Spring by (Wemto)

(a Pimbi is a hyrax, a small burrowing animal)

In the spring, the farmer plants seeds and little plants in the ground. Rain and sun help them grow.

Millie lives with her grandpa in an underground house among the rocks.

One day, Millie was reading a book. Something went drip, drip, drip. "What is dripping on my head?" asked Millie.

Grandpa said, "I don't know. Let's see why it is wet in here." The two went up and took a look around. Grandpa said, "See, it is raining and here is a hole in our house. It rains in the hole, and so it gets wet in the house. I will have to work on that hole."

"Now I see why rain makes it into the house," Millie said. She looked away and asked, "Who is that?"

"That is a farmer," Grandpa said. "He is putting little plants in the ground. The rain will help them grow."

Then Millie said, "Let's go! Here comes more rain. I don't want to get wet." Millie ran to the house, but Grandpa walked, as he was too fat to run.

When Grandpa came in, he said, "Millie, you did not get wet."

Millie said, "No, but more water is dripping down the hole. Drip, drip, drip. This time I will not get wet. I will keep my coat on."

The next day, Millie asked, "Grandpa, is it a wet day? Will the water drip in the hole? Will it get wet in here?"

Grandpa said, "No, it is not a wet day. The sun is out."

Taking her hat, Millie said, "Let's go up to see if the farmer is out. I want to see the farmer working."

They went up to see the farmer. "This is not the same farmer. Why is this farmer putting seeds in the ground?" asked Millie.

Grandpa said, "Plants will grow from the seeds in the ground."

Millie looked at the ground. "What is the farmer growing?"

Grandpa said, "We will see, but now I need to sleep."

Grandpa went to his room to sleep. Millie put on her hat, sat in the hot sun, and looked at the ground where the farmer planted seed.

She said, "Now I will see when plants grow out of the ground. Grow, little seeds, grow."

After his nap, Grandpa said, "Millie, come back to the house now. I must work on that hole."

"But Grandpa, I want to see when plants grow out of the ground."

"Millie, let's go back to the house. I will find some sunflower seeds for you to plant."

Millie was excited that Grandpa would find some seeds for her to plant next to the house. Millie planted the seeds, just like the farmer did.

The days were hot and the sun bright in the sky. The plants grew in the farmer's field. Millie looked where she planted her sunflower seeds. Millie exclaimed, "Grandpa, look! I have a big sunflower plant just like the farmer."

Grandpa made a watering can for Millie to water her plants. Millie watered and took care of her plants and they grew and grew.

"In the fall, the farmers picked their corn. They keep the corn over the winter for food," Grandpa said. "Come with me, Millie. I have something to show you."

The sky was bright and shining. It was a wonderful day. Millie asked, "Is this the day we will eat some sunflower seeds? Let's go to the sunflower field!"

Millie ran to the sunflower field. She saw a bird flying and called to the bird, "You come, too. I will give you some of my seeds to eat."

In the field, Grandpa picked a wonderful sunflower with ripe seeds. The three, Grandpa, Millie and the bird, sat in the bright sun eating Millie's sunflower seeds. "What a wonderful day," said Millie. Later, they harvested all of Millie's sunflowers.

The next day, Grandpa came into the kitchen. He said, "It is raining, again. The sky is not bright and my coat is all wet. We must stay inside today, but we have some wonderful sunflower seeds to eat." Millie went to get the jar of seeds from the kitchen shelf.

Millie said, "We have a shelf of glass jars of sunflower seeds, just like the farmers have."

Grandpa said, "Millie, you did a wonderful job of growing sunflowers. Now we will have jars of tasty sunflower seeds until next planting season. Now I need to sleep. Will you sing to me?"

The Old Man by Joy Relin

Once upon a time there lived an old man named Nguu. He lived in Molondoni Village in Machakos District. He was a very hard-working man. He was well known and loved by all who lived in his village. He was a kind man. Nguu had three sons who were noted for their laziness. They did not care about themselves or anyone else. They were exactly the opposite of their father.

In vain, Nguu tried to show them the advantages of hard work. Time and again, he told them that hard work pays, but they always turned a deaf ear to their father's advice. As Nguu grew older and older, he worried more and more about his sons' future. Sorrowfully, he thought to himself, "When I am dead, my name will be worthless, with three sons such as these."

One day Nguu felt ill and it was clear that he would not see the next season. As he lay in his bed waiting for death, he thought only of one thing: how his home would look after he had gone from this world.

Suddenly he had an idea, and after thinking it over for some time, he decided to put it into practice. He called his sons to him and said to them, "Now, my sons, I'm sorry but I forgot to tell you that there is a treasure hidden somewhere in my land. I should have remembered earlier, and then I could have shown you the exact spot. But now I'm weak. I can neither see nor walk. My advice to you is to dig up all the shamba (cultivated plot of land) and surely the treasure will be revealed to you." Shortly after, the old man died.

When they heard this, the sons quickly snatched anything they came across, pangas (machete), djembes (fork hoe) and shovels and ran to start work immediately. In a few weeks, they had finished digging up all the shamba. But to their disappointment, they did not see a sign of the treasure. They cursed their dead father.

"Now, here we are, brothers. We wasted our time and energy digging the land in search of the hidden treasure, but we have nothing. What shall we do?"

None of them seemed able to think of the next step. They were all equally disappointed. The oldest brother suggested that they plant the field. "If the rain falls well, then we may have a good yield," he said.

That season the rains were good and good crops were obtained. The brothers sold this produce for a good price and made a lot of money. They realized that their father had tricked them. There was no treasure in the shamba but the treasure produced by hard work!

A Disobedient Hunter by Kelvin Mnang'at

A long time ago people lived peacefully in the forest. They worshiped Thunder, the god of the skies. Thunder loved his people and provided them with everything they needed. There were many kinds of animals and birds for them to hunt and eat.

For many years the people lived happily. They obeyed Thunder and took care of him. The young men were trained to use their bows and arrows only for hunting. Thunder, however, warned the people that they should never kill any multicolored bird.

One day a group of young men went out to hunt. Among them was an expert hunter called Wango. Wango was proud and stubborn. The hunters killed enough animals and were on their way home when they stopped near a pool to drink water. While they were drinking, they saw a reflection of a very beautiful bird in the water.

"Look!" one hunter called out. "What a beautiful bird is in the water!"

"Is it really a bird?" Wango asked. "It has four legs and its head is very big. I've never seen such a strange bird." They all looked up and saw the most beautiful but the strangest bird they had ever seen. It was perched on a tree above the pool. The colors of its feathers were many and they looked like a rainbow.

The hunters could not believe their eyes. They thought they were dreaming. "That creature can't be a bird," Wango said. "Have you ever seen a bird with four legs? We should shoot it. Perhaps its meat is very tasty." With that he aimed his arrow at the bird.

As if it could understand what the hunters were saying, the bird flew lower down the tree and looked at them. The hunters realized that apart from its beauty and size, the bird had very bright eyes that looked at them strangely. They were afraid and tried to persuade Wango not to shoot it. Wango did not listen.

Wango told his fellow hunters that they were cowards. He shot his arrow, but neither he nor the other hunters lived to tell whether it hit the bird or not. In the twinkling of an eye, they were all struck by lightning. A deafening thunder and very heavy rain followed. It rained so hard that many people died.

The creature Wango had tried to shoot at was the son of Thunder. Thunder was so annoyed with the people's disobedience that he sent old age, sickness, poisons, and accidents. Since Wango shot at the son of Thunder, people have died and the people of the valley are no longer happy.

A Terrifying Experience by Denis Pkiach

Mario Musa had often heard it said that fire is a good steward but a bad master. Usually he would brush off such slogans as alarmist. Then came the day he frightfully learned the truth of the saying in black and white. It actually began as a minor incident like most fires do, but turned into a terrifying experience.

It was on a Saturday afternoon when Mario was all alone at home. His younger brother and two sisters had gone to play with children of the neighboring homestead. To while the day away, he sat down under a shady tree reading a thrilling book. His mind became absorbed in the story that he was reading.

He remembered that he had some science work to do: a chemistry experiment of all things. But the temptation to continue reading the story was almost irresistible. Couldn't the homework wait until later? Nonetheless, Mario reluctantly put down the book and decided to hurriedly carry out the experiment.

When Mario was rushing to the kitchen, he slipped on a puddle of water, which he had forgotten to clean, and found himself skidding on the floor. The mishap did not leave him unscathed. He hurt his ankle. Mario then limped across the room for some medicine.

Mario then tried to find his homemade burner to do the science experiment. He impatiently tried to locate his burner, and not without a little incensed mood. After failing to trace the burner, Mario got hold of his salt solution and switched on the cooker. What he didn't realize was that he had switched the cooker on full. Then Mario went back to his book and left the solution boiling, hoping to be back in a few minutes.

The part he was reading became more and more exciting. Soon he forgot about the experiment when, in the book, an investigator, who had gotten himself tied up with rope in a locked room and a time bomb in the corner ready to blow up any minute. Can the inspector get away before the bomb blows, then...? Suddenly, Mario heard a loud bang go off somewhere in the kitchen. Within a fraction of a second it occurred to Mario that the bomb had actually exploded, killing the poor inspector. Then Mario remembered the experiment.

Mario threw his book aside and ran to the kitchen where he found smoke billowing from the cooker. He was shaken and frightened even as he tried to turn off the switches and inspect for the damages. Fortunately there was nothing amiss with the cooker.

Mario quickly removed all traces of the burnt solution and cleaned up the messed-up place before his parents would arrive home from work. There was no denying that the situation could have been far worse and that a certain disaster had been averted by sheer luck. From that day, Mario resolved always to do one thing at a time and at least to read storybooks only after finishing all other work.

Experience Is The Best Teacher by Cornelius Poriot

"I wonder what Aoko is doing at home?" Njeri asked, looking at her friend Cherono. "Why don't we go and find out?"

The three were close friends: in fact inseparable. They spent most of the day together, especially during the school holidays, like now. Nine o'clock always found the girls together, and they would not part till evening. Strangely today, Aoko was nowhere to be seen; yet it was already ten o'clock.

The two girls walked to Aoko's house. As they neared the house, Njeri called out, "Aoko, you have a visitor." There was no response. Obviously, their friend was not in.

Outside the house was seated an old lady the two girls had never seen before. They went up to her and Cherono greeted her in Aoko's mother tongue. Cherono spoke the language fluently and one could not tell she was from a different community. The old lady responded and smiled broadly, exposing toothless gums. Njeri guessed the old lady was probably a hundred years old. Cherono then asked her where Aoko was.

"I sent her to the shop to buy something. Just come in and wait. I'm sure she's on her way back," said the old lady. Njeri did not understand a word. She just followed her friend into the house. Half an hour later, the girls were still waiting. Impatience got the better of Njeri. She suggested they go away and return later. Cherono, on the other hand had a different idea. She was curious about the old lady outside.

"Why don't we go out and chat with the old lady. You know these old people usually have fascinating stories to tell," reflected Cherono.

"But I won't understand a thing. For you the language is not a problem, so you will probably enjoy the stories," grumbled Njeri.

After a little persuasion, Njeir gave in on condition that Cherono would translate everything into English or Kiswahili.

They went out and found the old lady humming a tune. She was in a world of her own, her face a picture of happiness. She did not seem to notice the two girls, who also did not want to break into her bliss.

"Oh!" She exclaimed when she realized she was being watched. "I really love singing. It's good for the soul. Do you also sing?"

Njeri looked at Cherono, expecting her to translate what the old lady had just said. "I see your friend does not understand our language," the old lady said in English. The two girls were taken aback. "I just wanted to find out whether you two also love to sing," the old lady said, looking at Njeri.

"Yes," replied Njeri, "But I did not know you spoke English.

The old lady let out a hearty laugh, once again exposing her

84

toothless gums. She went on to explain that she was a retired teacher of English, having taught for forty years. "I was taught the language by its owners," she boasted.

"Just as I learned your language from its owners," Cherono remarked proudly. It was the old lady's turn to be astonished. "You mean you do not come from our community, yet you speak our language so well?"

Aoko arrived to find the three deep in conversation. She was holding a newspaper. She explained she had to walk all the way to the shopping center for it. "My great grandma loves reading, and as soon as she arrived here this morning, she asked for a newspaper."

Soon afterwards, the three girls skipped away leaving the old lady buried in the paper.

The Believed Dream by Marion Nelima

Once there was a poor man who had five children. The children were so small it was hard for him to care for them, so his wife was very hard working, like an ant that builds its house. The man was also hard working, but his wife worked even harder.

Every morning she would wake up and prepare food for her family. One day, while she was busy preparing food for the family, her oldest son shouted, "I am a doctor."

Then the father said, "You, a small child like you, a doctor?" The child answered, "Yes. When I was sleeping, I dreamt of being a doctor. I dreamt that many people were lying down from a plane crash. Then me, I was a flying doctor. When we were passing there up in the air, I realized that I could help them. In my mind, I thought, the people up in the air are the same as us and they breathe the same air. Because they are the same people, I, a doctor can help them."

Then his father said to him, "What a curious dream. I want you to read very hard in your studies so that you can pull up our life. You being our first born, we will need help from you. You have seen our life, how it looks."

Then the child answered, "Yes, I will put more effort in my studies."

When the boy was in class eight, he got a sponsorship and the boy tried very much. When he did his K.C.P.E (Kenya Certificate of Primary Education), he scored four hundred and thirty out of an effective maximum of 450.

His sponsor sent him to Australia, where he studied very hard and finished. When he came back home, everybody was very proud of him. His younger sisters and brothers were also in school and he was their example of what hard work can do.

He was still young looking in size but in age he was twenty-three.

He told everyone about his dream and his belief in education. His parents could sit down because their son had helped them out of poverty.

"This is very good you have pulled us out of poverty. Look, you have built for us a brick house. We used to live in a thatched house. We only thank you, our son, for listening to our advice. You are now a famous doctor."

ABOUT THE AUTHORS

8th grade students at Daylight School in Kapenguria, Kenya wrote the stories in this book, with one exception, the story by Michael Kimpur. Kapenguria is in West Pokot County, which is about 210 miles (338km) north of Nairobi, near the Uganda border. The school campus overlooks the Great Rift Valley with Mt. Elgon to the west.

The students at Daylight School are either orphans or very poor, not able to afford to go to school. Students of all religions, tribes and special needs are welcome. Most of the students come from nomadic, herding cultures including the Pokot, Turkana, and Karamoja tribes of west Kenya and east Uganda. Many are the first in their family to go to school.

Grades at the school run from pre-K to 8th grade. At the end of 8th grade, in December, students all over Kenya take a standardized test, in English, to determine if they are eligible for high school. For the students of Daylight School, English is their third language after their tribal language and Swahili. The test is difficult, the competition keen, but in 2015, all of the Daylight 8th grade students passed, with an average score placing the school among the leaders of the county. The 2016 class will be the second Daylight Class to take the test and the bar has been set high.

Like 8th grade students everywhere, they enjoy playing games, soccer, and just "hanging-out" with each other, but studies always come first. At school, they have a home, friends, food, and dreams of a wonderful future. Without the school, they wouldn't.

Made in the USA
San Bernardino, CA
31 October 2018